Boris Is Missing!

And Other Really Good Reasons to PRAY

Written and illustrated by
Sandy Silverthorne

Chariot Victor Publishing
A Division of Cook Communications

To Vicki,
my wife, best friend, and crown.

Chariot Victor Publishing
a division of Cook Communications,
Colorado Springs, Colorado 80918
Cook Communications, Paris, Ontario
Kingsway Communications, Eastbourne, England

BORIS IS MISSING!
© 1999 by Sandy Silverthorne for text and illustrations

Designed by Keith Sherrer
Edited by Kathy Davis

First hardcover printing, 1999
Printed in the United States of America
03 02 01 00 99   5 4 3 2 1

Library of Congress Cataloging-in-Publication Data

Silverthorne, Sandy, 1951-
      Boris is missing! : and other really good reasons to pray /
by Sandy Silverthorne.
         p.   cm.
      Summary: Confronted with a missing snake, a friend who is moving,
and an oral report, three kids find that prayer works because God
wants to be close to them and show them his love.
     ISBN 0-7814-3240-5
     [1. Prayer—Fiction.]   I. Title.
PZ7.S5884Bo 1999
[E] — dc21

                                98-55700
                                  CIP

At 7 A.M. there really was no hint of just how bad things were going to get. The sun was shining, the birds were singing, and Gregory hadn't gotten into trouble once.

Of course, he was still fast asleep.

Gregory's normal routine was to get up, wash his face, check on Boris the class snake, then head down to breakfast. So this morning he got up, washed his face, noticed that Boris wasn't in his cage, and headed down to . . .

. . . whoa!

What's this?

Boris isn't in his cage!?!!

After that discovery,

things started heading downhill fast.

"Where can he be? How did he get out?" Gregory asked.

He ran through the house looking everywhere . . .

. . . in the lamps,

under the sofa,

in the closets—even in the toaster.

Gregory had promised Miss Fronebush, his second-grade teacher, that he would be responsible and take good care of Boris.

He'd had Boris only three days!

Now what would he do?

People often told Gregory he didn't take good care of things, and this was his chance to prove them wrong.

Maybe.

"You should put up signs around the neighborhood," suggested Gregory's dad.

"That won't work," said Gregory.
"Boris can't read English."

As it so happens, Gregory wasn't the only one with a problem.

At that very moment in the yellow house two blocks away, Bradley was having the worst day he'd had since he cut his toe on the slide at school and had to get a tetanus shot.

You see, Bradley's best friend, Tyler, was moving the next day—**all the way to Redwillow Lane!**

That had to be <u>at</u> <u>least</u> a mile and a half away!

Tyler had lived across the street since he and Bradley
were little. Bradley knew he had to do something to
stop this madness, but what?

He could hide Tyler in the exercise room—no one
ever goes in there.

Or ...

... he could figure out a way to stall
the moving truck long enough to
whisk Tyler safely out of town!

Meanwhile, halfway between Bradley's house and the school, Christy was just waking up. You know how it is when you're still drowsy and it's so nice 'cause you don't remember that you've got a big scary thing to do today.

Christy's **big scary thing** was to stand up in front of the whole class and give her oral report on the Netherlands.

She hated speaking in front of the class—she got so NERVOUS.

All three of the kids had to get to school, so they headed to the one place where they could come together for direction and wisdom …

… the playground.

PLAYGROUND RULES

☐ Thou shalt not throw rocks.

☐ Thou shalt share.

☐ Thou shalt put the balls away when you're done.

Normy and his sister Marpel (the know-it-all) came along and quickly joined in the discussion.

Marpel was quick to give her ideas.

What you need to do is to <u>worry</u> about it...
<u>then</u> take matters into your own hands...

Normy had an idea too.

Pray? **About *this* stuff?**

They knew they could pray for mom and dad and grandma and grandpa and for the food, but pray about a missing snake, a moving friend, and a speech on the Netherlands?

Marpel was the first to speak.

"Pray? **Good idea.** I'll start."

(She'd heard them talk like this in the film version of *The Ten Commandments*.)

"I think when you pray you just talk to God," Normy said. "You don't have to use fancy words or try to sound right. **Just tell Him what's on your heart.**"

"Sounds good to me," Christy said.

"Lord, You know how I hate to talk in front of people, so would You make it so I don't have to do it, please? Have the lights go out, or the teacher forget me, or the hallways flood—or something."

"And Lord, if You don't make Tyler move, I'll clean my room every hour, and I'll be nice to my brother, and I won't talk in class, and I'll remember to brush my teeth, and I won't throw rocks."

"Lord, if I can't find Boris, I don't know what I'll do.

Will You find him, please?"

"Amen."

And you know what? God answered all three prayers—but not **exactly** in the ways Christy, Bradley, and Gregory expected.

He didn't rescue Christy from giving her speech, but He helped her get through it.

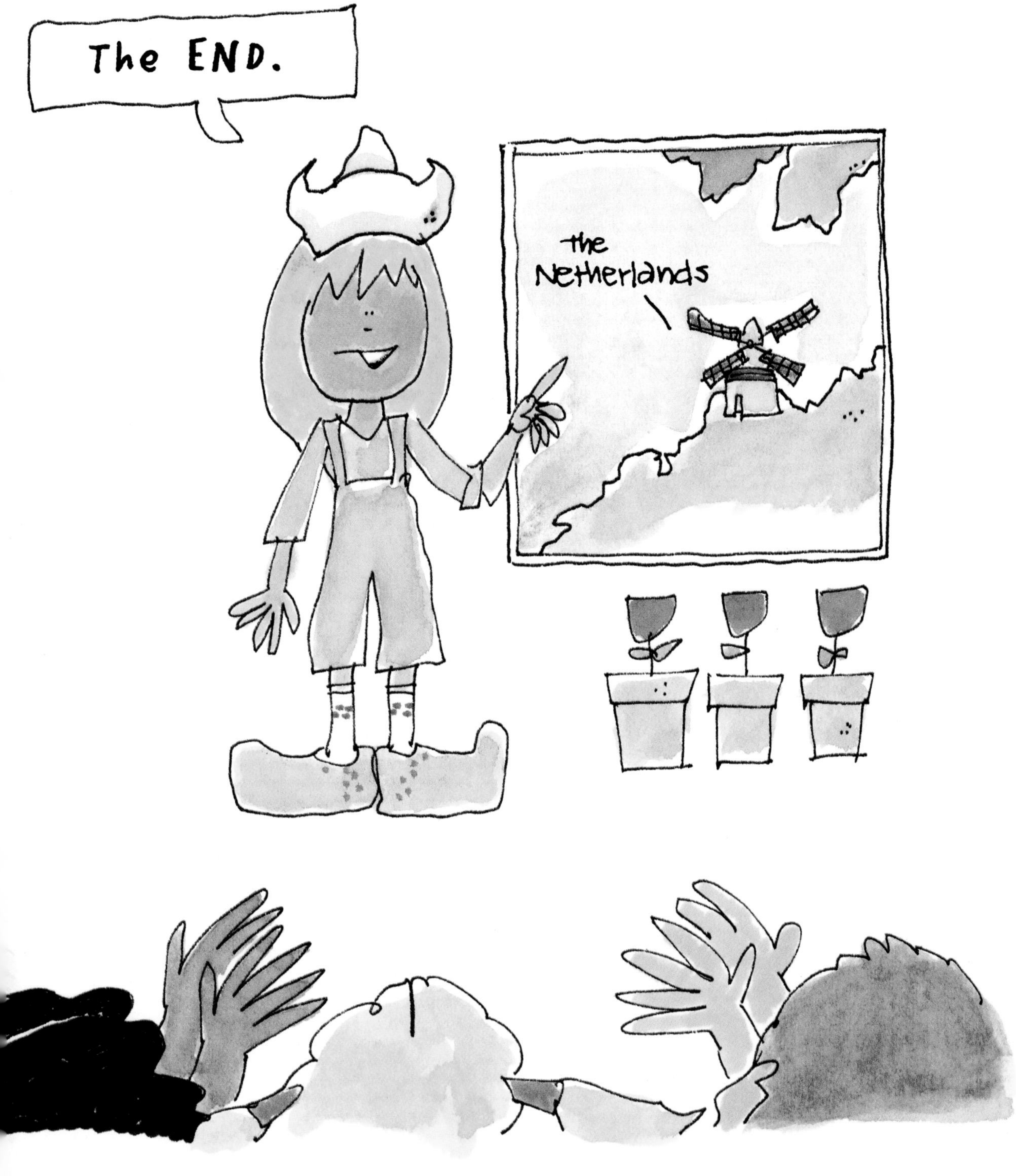
The END.
the Netherlands

And Tyler still moved away, but he came back to see Bradley the very first day. And he told him all about his new house, and the tree fort, and that his mom said Bradley could come over any time.

But poor Gregory.

Still no sign of Boris....

Was he gone for good?

What would Gregory tell the teacher...

...and the class?

Does God care about Gregory?

So God found Boris, He helped Christy do her report on the Netherlands, and He took care of the Tyler situation.

BUT… best of all, He taught these three kids that He wants to be close to them in all that they do because… **He loves them!**

In fact, God likes it when they talk to Him
even when they're not having a problem.

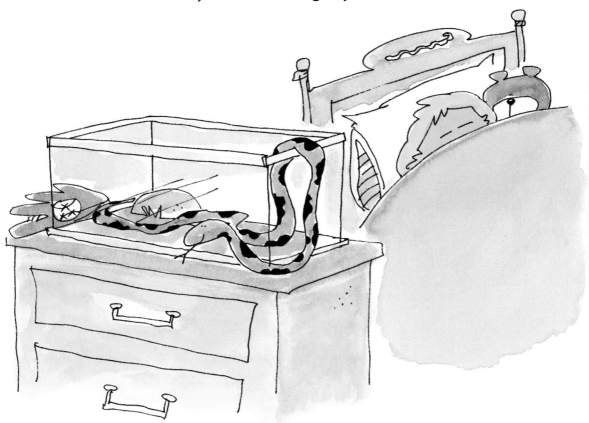

So everyone learned something today.

That is, everyone **except Boris,** who
apparently didn't learn anything at all
from this experience.

Faith Parenting Guide

Boris Is Missing!
And Other Really Good Reasons to Pray

Ages: 4-7

Life Issue: My child doesn't understand that prayer is simply talking to God throughout the day.

Spiritual Building Block: Prayer

Learning Styles

Visual Learning Style: After reading the story, help your child make a list of prayer requests for your family. Give your child a piece of poster paper and let him cut pictures out of old magazines and paste them on the paper or draw pictures to represent each of the prayer requests. Help him label each request, and pray with him about one request each day.

Auditory Style: Discuss the different reasons for prayer that are demonstrated in the story. For example, Gregory had lost something important and needed help finding it; Bradley was sad and needed help adjusting to a new situation; Christy needed help getting through a scary task. Ask your child to think of something that's happening in her life right now that's similar to one of these situations. Discuss ways she can pray about the problem and specific things she might say to God. Offer to pray with your child about it.

Tactile Learning Style: Using the furniture in your home, create an obstacle course. Blindfold one of your children and have him ask another child (or you) to guide him through the course using voice commands. Give all family members a turn. (Change the course before each round so the kids can't memorize the course, but must depend on the guide.) After everyone has had a turn, ask:

- What made it easy or hard for you to go through the maze?
- How do you think this game relates to prayer?

Say: "To get through this maze you had to listen to the voice of someone who could see the maze. To get through the maze of life you need to listen to what God is telling you. The maze is like God's plan for your life. You can't see it all, but God can. If you stop talking to God and listening for His guidance, you won't know where to go next. Prayer is a way to keep in constant contact with God."

The tactile learning activity is adapted from *Family Night Tool Chest: Christian Character Qualities,* by Jim Weidmann and Kurt Bruner with Mike and Amy Nappa, 1998, Chariot Victor Publishing, pp. 63-64.